A ROOKIE READER

WAIT, SKATES!

By Mildred D. Johnson

Illustrations by Tom Dunnington

Prepared under the direction of Robert Hillerich, Ph.D.

CHILDRENS PRESS ™

CHICAGO

Library of Congress Cataloging in Publication Data

Johnson, Mildred D. (Mildred Dawes)
   Wait! skates.

   (Rookie reader)
   Includes index.
   Summary: A child putting on roller skates for the first time finally teaches them to wait.
   [1. Roller skating—Fiction]   I. Dunnington, Tom, ill.
II. Title.   III. Series.
PZ7.J63416Wai   1983   [E]   82-22228
ISBN 0-516-02039-0

12 13 14 15 16 17 R 94 93 92

Wait!

4

Wait, skates!

The first time on my roller skates,

I tried to make my skates wait.

But, they would not wait.

They went out

13

and sometimes in.

They would not wait.

They would not go straight.

But, I just stopped

21

and said out loud…

Wait!

Wait, skates. Wait!

Now I just sail along.

My skates go straight.

WORD LIST

			straight
			the
along	just	out	they
and	loud	roller	time
but	make	said	to
first	my	sail	tried
go	not	skates	wait
I	now	sometimes	went
in	on	stopped	would

About the Author

   Mildred D. Johnson is a native of Baltimore, Maryland. Moving to Chicago over twenty-five years ago, she established a children's theater and continued her teaching career at Howalton School, the oldest Black private school in Chicago. She also served as a provisional teacher in the Chicago public schools. She has conducted numerous in-service workshops for teachers and organized many creative assemblies.

   Mrs. Johnson is a playwright, and the author of a number of children's books. She conducted her children's theater **SAY** for fourteen years, writing and producing its yearly musical play. She has written for **Ebony Jr!** since its inception in 1973. She endeavors to publish material that will enlighten Black children and young adults.

   Mrs. Johnson holds a Bachelor's Degree from the National College of Education, and a Master's Degree in Language and Speech from Governors State University where she was the recipient of a Writer's Scholarship.

About the Artist:

   Tom Dunnington divides his time between book illustration and wildlife painting. He has done many books for Childrens Press, as well as working on textbooks, and is a regular contributor to "Highlights for Children." Tom lives in Oak Park, Illinois.